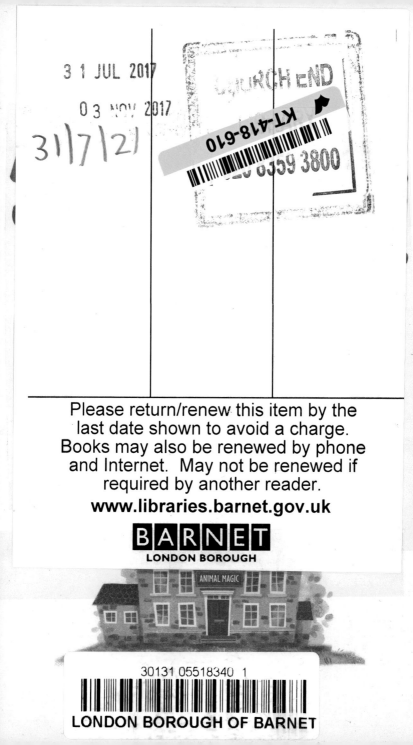

Please return/renew this item by the
last date shown to avoid a charge.
Books may also be renewed by phone
and Internet. May not be renewed if
required by another reader.

www.libraries.barnet.gov.uk

BARNET
LONDON BOROUGH

ANIMAL MAGIC

This series is for my riding friend Shelley,
who cares about all animals.

STRIPES PUBLISHING
An imprint of Little Tiger Press
1 The Coda Centre, 189 Munster Road, London SW6 6AW

A paperback original
First published in Great Britain in 2006
This edition published in 2016

Text copyright © Jenny Oldfield, 2006, 2016
Inside Illustrations copyright © Artful Doodlers, 2016
Cover illustration copyright © Anna Chernyshova, 2016
Images courtesy of www.shutterstock.com

ISBN: 978-1-84715-680-8

A CIP catalogue record for this book is available from the British Library.

Printed and bound in the UK

10 9 8 7 6 5 4 3 2 1

ANIMAL RESCUE

The Home-alone Kitten

TINA NOLAN

Stripes

ANIMAL MAGIC
RESCUE CENTRE

🏠 HOME

💜 ADOPT

✋ FRIENDS

MEET THE ANIMALS IN NEED OF A HOME!

APACHE

7-year-old piebald, 13.1 hands, Apache is looking for a keen rider who will hack him out in company or alone.

LIBBY

We don't know Libby's age, and she won't look her best until her clipped fur grows back ... but she'll love you to bits!

PENNY

A two-year-old Border collie cross with bags of energy. Can you play ball with her and give her all the walks she needs?

NEWS

HELP US

CONTACT

£ DONATE!

SATIN

A beautiful
5-year-old Siamese
who would like you
to fuss and pamper
her. She needs to
be an only pet.

BECKS

A 4-year-old
Great Dane and
a friendly giant!
He needs a very
special home with
plenty of room to
stretch his legs!

KITTENS

One adorable litter
is 10 weeks old.
You'll fall in love
with Treacle, Snap
and Wilma the
moment you see
them!

Chapter One

"'Animal Magic – we match the perfect pet with the pefect owner!'"

Eva Harrison read the words on the computer screen. "You missed out the 'r' in the second 'perfect'," she pointed out to her brother, Karl. They'd been working together for almost an hour, designing a leaflet for Animal Magic's Open Day.

Karl added the 'r' and scrolled through the rest of the leaflet. "Can I print it off now?" he asked.

"Just a minute." Eva read the whole thing over again. "'We take in and care for unwanted animals and rehome them with caring owners.' Yep, cool. 'We make sure that no healthy animal is ever put to sleep.' Yeah, that's good. 'In our first year we rehomed 124 dogs and 156 cats. We also found new owners for five horses, two goats, plus forty-two rabbits and thirteen guinea pigs.'" She looked at the photos underneath. There was one of three feral kittens, Treacle, Wilma and Snap, and another of a white rabbit called Pom-Pom. "Cute!" she murmured.

"So can I print it?" Karl asked impatiently.

"Wait!" Eva read on. "'Animal Magic Open Day. Saturday 5th August. Meet a celeb!' This is the best bit! 'Soccer star,

Jake Adams, will be here to meet you on Saturday at 2.00 p.m. Jake and his girlfriend, Marietta, are big fans of Animal Magic, so don't miss your chance to chat and get Jake's autograph!' Can you believe it!"

"I know, this really is cool!" Karl agreed, clicking the mouse to begin printing the leaflets. He and his best mate, George Stevens, were seriously into football. "I can't wait to meet Jake!"

"I already have," Eva reminded him. It wasn't often that she had one up on her older brother, but this time she did. "I was with Dad when he took Charlie to Jake's house, remember."

"Yeah, no need to rub it in," Karl muttered, keeping an eye on the printer as it churned out the leaflets.

Eva sailed on regardless. "Jake lives at Okeham Hall, a massive mansion with a swimming pool. He came to the door with Marietta. I handed him Charlie and he said thanks. He said we were doing a great job."

"Yeah, yeah!" Karl sniffed. "Next you'll be telling me that it was you who persuaded him to come to our Open Day!"

"Yeah well, no, actually, that was down to Dad." Eva had to admit the truth. "Jake invited us in. That was when Dad asked him to be our last-minute celebrity guest. Jake said yeah, he'd love to do it if it helps to raise our pro-feel—"

"Raise our what?" Karl cut in.

"Pro-feel – y'know, if it helps make us more well known."

"You mean *profile*!" Karl grinned.

"Whatever." Taking a stack of leaflets fresh from the printer, Eva blushed and made a quick exit. "Only two days to go!" she muttered. "I'd better post these through every letter box in the village."

"Here, take another *peel*!" Karl laughed. "And remember, take it easy – delivering those leaflets means you'll have to walk *meels* and *meels*!"

"Hah!" Eva retorted, flouncing off to the surgery to find their mum.

"Hi, Dad. Is Mum about?" Eva asked, popping her head around the office door. "Is she in the surgery?"

Her dad looked up from his pile of papers. "She's in the stables, vaccinating the two ponies we brought in yesterday."

Eva hurried on past the surgery and the row of converted barns that housed the smaller rescue animals until she came to the small block of new stables that her dad had been working on for the last few weeks. "Mum?" she called, stepping out of the sunlight into the stables.

"Hush!" Heidi whispered. She was stroking the neck of a small brown and

white pony whose shaggy mane fell over
his dark eyes. "Apache didn't like his
injection, did you, boy?"

"Aah! But it'll make you feel better,"
said Eva, scratching Apache's nose.
Quietly, she went up to the other pony,
a skinny chestnut called Rosie. "Do you
want a stroke, too?" she murmured.

Rosie nuzzled Eva's palm with her soft nose. Inside the stall, a hay-net hung from the wall and there was a bucket of feed on the floor.

"We'll soon feed you up and make you big and strong!" Eva promised, remembering the parched field where they had found her. A neighbour had called Animal Magic to say that the poor creature had been left without fresh water and abandoned by her owners while they took a two-week holiday in Spain.

"Hey, Apache," Heidi whispered, still stroking the little piebald. "Now that needle didn't really hurt, did it?" She turned to Eva. "Did you want something?" she reminded her.

"Oh yeah. We've finished the leaflets

about the Open Day. I wanted to ask if I can deliver them round the village."

"Let me see."

Eva handed her mum a leaflet. Heidi read through it, nodding and finally saying, "Yes, that's fine. It looks very good… Eva, did you hear me?"

"Hmm?" Eva had her arms around Rosie's neck and she was murmuring sweet nothings into the pony's ear. "Oh, yeah. Thanks, Mum!"

Heidi smiled. "Go!" she urged.

"OK, I'm out of here!" Eva said. "Here I come, Okeham village!"

Chapter Two

Eva hurried up Main Street, pushing leaflets through letter boxes, humming as she went. She felt really excited about Saturday. All the plans were going well, especially since Jake Adams had agreed to be there.

"Hi, George. Are you coming on Saturday?" she called to Karl's best mate, who stood astride his bike in his driveway. She fluttered a leaflet under his face. "You'll get to meet Jake Adams!"

"Wow, no way! Is this for real?"

Eva nodded. "So you'll come?" She was already on her way.

"Count me in," George said. He cycled after Eva to the house next door. "What time does Jake arrive?"

"Two o'clock!" she called over her shoulder. "Be there early if you want to get his autograph!"

"Our big day will soon be here!" Eva told Treacle, Snap and Wilma, one of four litters of kittens in the cattery. Charlie was their brother, and as yet, he was the only one to find a perfect new home.

"We'll have to make you look extra specially beautiful on Saturday," she

cooed, lifting out ten-week-old Treacle and tickling his tummy.

The brown tabby wriggled and squirmed.

"Yes, I know, you're already adorable!" Eva laughed. Her dad had found the litter in an air vent at the back of a factory. Realizing that they were wild, and seemingly without their mum, he had brought them back to Animal Magic. Eva had given the four kittens names before Jake Adams had come along and taken Charlie.

"There'll be hundreds of people," she promised, putting Treacle back into the kitten unit then moving on to check a Siamese stray called Satin. Right now the cattery was bursting at the seams with animals needing owners, just like the dog kennels next door.

"Hundreds of people!" Eva repeated, as she closed the cattery door and went into the kennels to see Penny, Bruno and Becks. "Down, Becks!" she said sternly to the black Great Dane.

Becks was almost as tall as Eva – a gentle giant who had been dumped at their door a month earlier. He gazed at her with soft brown eyes that would melt the hardest heart.

"*Hundreds!*" she promised, going from one kennel to the next.

The dogs woofed and whined. They jumped up and wagged their tails.

"People will queue for Jake Adams's autograph then they'll come to visit you," she told them. "They'll see you and fall in love with you. Before you know it, they'll want to take you home."

"Woof!" the dogs replied. "Woof – wruff – woof!"

Eva looked up at the pink sky as the sun disappeared in the west. "It's going to be the best, *best* day!"

Chapter Three

"Hi, Eva. Can I come in?" Annie Brooks poked her head around the cattery door.

It was early Friday morning, and Eva was feeding the cats. "Sure. Why not?"

Annie bit her lip nervously. "I wondered if you were still talking to me, after what Mum and Dad have done."

Eva smiled. "We're not at war with you, Annie. Only your mum and dad!"

"I'm so sorry!" Annie sighed. She sidled up to the kitten unit where

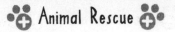

Treacle, Snap and Wilma snoozed in
the warmth. "You know what Mum's
like. She's always joining committees
and setting up campaigns against stuff.
Last year it was to stop cars speeding
through the village."

"And this year it's to close us down,"
said Eva. "But why doesn't she like us?"
she asked, placing a bowl of food in
front of a white cat called Libby. Libby's
long coat had been so filthy and matted
that Heidi had decided to clip it off,
except for the fur on her face and tail.
Now she looked strange and scrawny as
she gobbled her food.

Annie shrugged. "She reckons you're
noisy and attract too much traffic, stuff
like that."

"Doesn't she care about animals?"

"Yes, she does. But she doesn't like having them next door, that's all." Annie wanted to change the subject, so she asked if she could pick up Wilma.

"Go ahead," Eva told her. "With any luck, by this time tomorrow, she might not be here!"

Annie nestled the tiny kitten against her. "So cute!" she murmured. Wilma meowed and cuddled up close. "Aah, have they found you a new home?"

"Not yet. But it's our Open Day tomorrow, so here's hoping!"

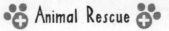

Annie frowned and put Wilma back
into the unit. She tucked a strand of
dark hair behind her ear. "What Open
Day?"

"Oh," Eva said, feeling embarrassed.
"Hmm, yeah – I was too scared to post
a leaflet through your letter box," Eva
explained. "I thought your mum might
tell me off. Anyway, we're inviting the
whole village to Animal Magic so they
can see what we do. Mum says it'll help
find new owners for all the animals."

"Hmm." Annie's frown deepened. "That
means lots of cars and lots of people.
Maybe I'd better break it to Mum."

"OK, if you think that's best," Eva
said. "But poor you!"

"Yeah, I'd better go," Annie decided,
heading for the door.

"Take a break," Heidi suggested when she saw Eva pushing a wheelbarrow towards the manure heap at the back of the yard. "Don't wear yourself out. It's going to be a long day."

"I'm fine!" Eva insisted, trundling on. "I want to finish mucking out."

Her mum waited at the stable door until Eva came back with an empty barrow. "Good job!" she smiled. "I just came to take a look at Apache, to make sure he's OK after yesterday's jab."

"Apache's fine," Eva said, following Heidi into the stables. "But take a look at Rosie. She's stomping around a bit and pawing the ground. She doesn't look very happy."

Heidi nodded. She looked at the little chestnut mare, who had now gone down on to her knees and was trying to roll on to her side inside her stall. "This doesn't look good," Heidi muttered, clicking into action. "Eva, fetch me a head collar. We need to get Rosie out of here and walking around the yard as quickly as possible."

Eva did as she was told. "What is it? What's wrong?" She held open the stable door as her mum buckled the head collar, got the pony back on to her feet, and then led her outside.

"It could be colic," Heidi replied. "If we've caught it early, she'll be OK."

Eva gasped and caught up with her mum. "And if not?" she asked.

"Colic is serious." Heidi didn't hide

the facts. "If we haven't got to her in time, I'm afraid Rosie could die!"

"Poor Rosie!" Karl exclaimed. He had seen what was happening from the kitchen window and run out to help. He took over the lead-rope from Heidi, who ran to fetch her vet's bag from the surgery.

Eva felt helpless as she watched the pony stiffen her legs and refuse to walk. Then Rosie turned her head towards her flank and curled her lip to show her teeth. "Mum, hurry. She looks as if she's in real trouble!"

Heidi ran back. She checked Rosie's symptoms. "Yes, she's sweating up, and her heart rate is racing. I'm pretty sure this is colic."

"Come on, girl," Karl urged.

"It's probably due to her change of diet," Heidi told them. She pressed her hands against Rosie's flank. "Yes, it feels like there's some kind of intestinal blockage. But if we keep walking her, it might clear itself."

"Walk on!" Eva begged.

"Yes. Come on, Rosie, you can do it!" Karl urged.

Gamely the little pony responded to their voices. She took a step forward, then another. Gradually she began to move around the yard.

"Good work!" Heidi told Karl and Eva. "Eva, keep talking to her. Karl, keep some pressure on the rope to lead her on."

"Does it hurt a lot?" Eva asked Heidi, who nodded. "It'll soon be better," Eva soothed.

"We hope!" Karl muttered.

Walking ahead of Rosie, Eva checked over her shoulder to see that the pony was still following. Out of the corner of her eye, she noticed Linda Brooks appear at the main gate. "Uh-oh!" she warned the others. "Here comes more trouble!"

"Everything OK?" Mark asked Eva. He'd called home in his lunch break. "Are we all ready for the big day?"

"Erm, actually not so good," Eva told him. "Rosie's got colic. Karl and I are taking it in turns to walk her round the yard."

"Oh no. How is she?" Her dad sounded worried.

"A bit better. Mum says it's probably a food blockage, so hopefully it's not going to be serious long-term. Her temperature's going down now."

"Good. What else?"

"Mrs Brooks came round."

"Uh-oh!" Mark knew this could only mean one thing. "What happened?"

"Annie told her about our Open Day. Mrs Brooks got really mad and yelled at Mum. Mum kept her cool and said she was busy with an emergency. Mrs Brooks said she'd call the police if cars blocked her drive. She stomped about a bit and then she went home."

"Oh dear," Mark said. "Maybe I'll pop round and see them when I finish work."

"One more thing," Eva added, to crown what had been a bad morning. "Karl listened to the weather forecast and it's not good. They say there's going to be a thunderstorm tomorrow and it'll pour with rain."

"Just what we need!" There was a long silence, and then her dad gave a deep sigh. "Never mind. Maybe things aren't going according to plan," he said. "But at least we still have the star turn of Jake Adams up our sleeves!"

"Don't give Rosie anything to eat until I say so," Heidi told Eva, before heading off to the surgery. A stray dog had just been brought in by one of the Animal Magic volunteers and it needed a full examination. "She can drink plenty of water, but no food!"

Eva nodded and stroked Rosie's nose. The sick pony was back in her stable, still shaking from the pain of her colic. But her temperature and pulse were back to normal. She was over the worst.

"Good girl!" Eva soothed as Rosie nuzzled her hand. "You're going to be fine, I promise."

Eva settled the pony into her fresh, clean stable. "*We're* going to be fine!" she told herself, getting over the morning's events. "Dad will sort things out with Mr and Mrs Brooks. The forecast will be wrong, and tomorrow will be a lovely sunny day. There'll be a huge crowd! And Jake Adams will be the star attraction!"

"I wouldn't count on it if I were you." Karl had wandered into the stable. There was a deep frown on his face.

"Uh-oh, it's Mr Grumpy!" Eva told Rosie. "Seems like he's in a bad mood. Don't take any notice."

Karl sniffed and went to stroke Apache.

"He gets like this," Eva explained brightly, as if Rosie understood every word. "Something probably went wrong with the website. Maybe he can't download a picture or perhaps he's deleted something by mistake."

Karl tutted and his mood darkened. "Shut up, Eva!"

She made a face behind his back. Then she felt bad for teasing him. "OK, OK, I'm sorry. Is something really wrong?"

Karl sighed, turned away and then strode back towards her. "We've had a message from Jake Adams," he told her.

Eva's heart did a little flip, and seemed to stop and then start again. "Saying what?" she whispered.

Karl looked her in the eyes and gave her the bad news. "Saying he can't come to the Open Day," he reported. "Something happened. He had to go away."

Eva gasped. She shook her head in disbelief.

"It's true," Karl insisted. "It's all off. Jake won't be here tomorrow. *Finito*. End of story. *Kaput*."

Chapter Four

"Jake didn't give a reason," Karl
insisted, shaking his head in disbelief.
"He just said he had to go away. I can
show you the email if you want. I tried
to send him a reply but it just bounced
back."

"No reasons and no apology?" Mark
checked. He'd come home early to
lend a hand with the preparations. "I'm
really surprised. I had Jake Adams
down as a decent sort of guy."

"Me too," Karl said gloomily.

"So now we have no celebrity." Heidi let out a long sigh. "And it's too late either to find someone else or to let people know."

Eva sat without saying a word. Mrs Brooks was on the warpath, it was going to rain, and now Jake couldn't come. Their big day lay in ruins.

"Maybe we should cancel the whole thing," Karl muttered.

"No, no, we have to go ahead," his dad argued. "Bear in mind that our main aim is to find new homes for our animals. It's a huge shame Jake's not coming, but people will still be able to look round the place and we can still match up pets with new owners just the same."

"But it *won't* be the same!" Karl insisted. "Everyone will be disappointed. What am I going to tell George when he shows up expecting to get Jake's autograph?"

"Dad's right," Heidi cut in. "We have to go ahead. Mark, do you want to go next door to calm Linda down, or shall I?"

Eva's dad got up from the table and headed for the door. "I'll do it."

Eva turned to Karl, who was still moping. "I want to look at Jake's email. Can I use the computer in your room?"

"Feel free." He followed Eva upstairs and quickly went online.

Eva frowned as she read the message.

From: Jake Adams
To: Animal Magic

Subject: Open Day

Message: Can't come tomorrow.
         Have to go away. Jake

She pressed the reply button and wrote, "Can Marietta still make it?" Then she pressed send. The message stayed in the outbox then came back unsent.

"See!" Karl sighed. "Anyway, what's the point?"

"Marietta would be better than no one," Eva replied. "She gets in all the celebrity magazines. She's always going to parties with famous people."

Karl nodded. "But if we can't send an email, we're stuck."

Eva frowned. She wasn't giving up that easily. "No we're not!" she replied, heading downstairs and into the yard with Karl racing behind.

"What are you doing? Where are you going?" Karl watched her grab her bike.

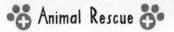

"I'm doing what people did before they had email. I'm going to cycle out to Okeham Hall and speak to Marietta!"

Karl's mouth dropped open. "Hey, wait! No, hang on!" He ran for his own bike and followed Eva on to Main Street.

"I'm coming too!" Karl called after her. "Eva, wait for me!"

Chapter Five

"O-o-oh, wow!" Karl stopped beside Eva at the gates of Okeham Hall. Karl had never seen the house before, even though he knew, like all the rest of the world, that Jake Adams and his girlfriend had recently moved in.

The soccer star's home was fairytale stuff – a massive old house with a long, tree-lined drive. It had square towers and big stone pillars. "Where's the swimming pool?" he asked.

"Round the back," Eva told him. "Marietta gave Dad and me a quick tour when we came to drop Charlie off."

Karl got off his bike and propped it against the wall. He inspected the fancy iron gates. "These gates are electronic and they're locked. What do we do now?"

"Press that button and speak into the microphone thingy?" Eva suggested.

Karl pressed, but nothing happened. "Looks like there's no one in. Come on, let's go."

"We're not going to give up that easily!" Starting to pedal again, Eva made her way cautiously along the road until she came to a narrow side lane. "Come on!" she called.

The lane was rough and overgrown

but, as Eva expected, it led down the side of Okeham Hall. A little way along she spotted what she'd been looking for.

"Look, there's a gate into the garden." Leaving her bike in some long grass, Eva went ahead and tested the handle. "And this one's open!"

She pushed the gate and stepped on to the soccer idol's smooth green lawn.

"Whoa, we could be in trouble here!" Karl pointed out. "This is trespassing."

Eva tutted. "I've been here before, remember. Marietta and Jake know me!"

Swallowing hard, Karl followed his sister across the wide lawn, and then past a bright blue open-air pool.

Eva led the way towards a door at the back of the old house and rang the bell. Once again there was no answer.

"Look, they've both gone away," Karl insisted, turning to go. "We're wasting our time. Come on."

"They can't have both gone," Eva protested. "What about Charlie?"

Karl shrugged. "What *about* Charlie?"

Eva peered through the glass panels of the door. "He only just came here. They wouldn't leave him home alone."

"Maybe a neighbour is looking after

him. Come on, Eva, let's go!"

As Eva carried on peering into the
house, Karl turned to see a small ginger
shape peep out from behind one of the
large flowerpots beside the door.

"Uh-oh!" he said, watching the fluffy
kitten emerge from his hiding place.
Charlie had a cute little face and two
white paws. "You shouldn't be outside
by yourself!"

Eva spun round and spotted him.
"So much for him being looked after by
a neighbour!" she muttered.

Scared and alone, the kitten began
to run. He darted between more plant
pots, charging helter-skelter towards the
swimming pool.

"Oh no!" Eva saw the danger and
began to run after Charlie. She tried to
cut him off, but he scooted between her
feet, under a poolside chair and … splash,
straight into the deep end of the pool!

Eva cried out as she watched poor
little Charlie sink beneath the surface.

A split second later Karl was racing
towards the pool. He plunged after the
kitten fully clothed.

Eva squeezed her eyes tight shut,
hardly daring to watch. When she

opened them again Karl had already
caught hold of Charlie, pulling him
back to the surface and holding him
clear of the water.

"Here!" he yelled at Eva. "Grab him!"

She knelt and leaned out over the
water to take the dripping kitten. "Are
you OK?" she asked Karl.

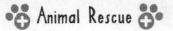

"Yes, don't worry about me. How's Charlie?"

The kitten meowed and shivered in her arms. Eva took off her jacket and quickly wrapped him in it. "He'll be fine."

As Karl hauled himself out of the pool, Eva rubbed the kitten dry. She felt his rough little tongue lick her hand and saw his bright green eyes peer out from the folds of her jacket. "Don't worry," she murmured. "You're safe now."

"And I'm dripping wet!" Karl groaned, taking off a trainer and emptying the water from it. "Honestly, Eva, I wish we'd never come!"

"Hush!" she told Charlie as he meowed and licked. "Of course it's a good job we came."

"Yeah, so we could scare the poor little thing and make him jump into the pool! Like, that was a really good thing!"

Eva sighed. "Look, there's no cat flap. If we hadn't come, Charlie would have been locked out and left all by himself. He could have fallen into the pool at any time, and there would have been no one around to rescue him!"

"Yeah, I see what you mean," Karl grunted, putting his shoes back on.

"How could Jake and Marietta leave him?" Eva said. "What were they thinking?" She made up her mind what they had to do and began to head back the way they'd come. "We can't leave Charlie here. We'll have to take him back to Animal Magic!"

Shaking his head like a dog drying itself, Karl ran after her. "Hang on! Let's just think this through."

But Eva didn't hesitate. "I'm not leaving Charlie home alone!" she insisted. "I don't care who Jake Adams is, or what he says, Charlie is coming back with us!"

Chapter Six

"So now we have the mystery of the vanishing soccer star *and* the home-alone kitten on our hands." Heidi had taken Rosie's temperature and checked her pulse. Both were back to normal and the pony stood comfortably in her stall.

"How could we get it so wrong in the first place?" Eva wondered. She stood with Charlie snuggled inside her jacket, fast asleep.

She and Karl had carried Charlie back from Okeham Hall and told their mum what had happened. Heidi had sent Karl inside to get changed into dry clothes.

"We followed our Animal Magic rules and we all thought Jake and Marietta were the perfect owners for the perfect pet!" Eva pointed out.

"We can't be right one hundred per cent of the time," her mum said. "Hello again, little cutie," she murmured, tickling Charlie's chin. "I hear you've just used up one of your nine lives!"

"But Mum, you said Jake seemed to love cats," Eva reminded her. "Marietta, too – you said she wanted to take the whole lot home!"

Taking Charlie from Eva, Heidi led

the way out of the stables towards the cattery. "But people sometimes promise things, then don't act on their promises. They mean well at the time, I suppose."

Heidi popped Charlie into the kitten unit that housed Treacle, Snap and Wilma. "Say hello to your brother!" she said with a smile.

The boldest of the kittens was Treacle, and he came forward to greet Charlie by sniffing and raising his front paw.

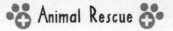

Charlie meowed and backed away, straight into Snap. Then Wilma pounced on Charlie and began to play-fight.

"Wilma loves you really!" Eva laughed, as Charlie entered into the rough and tumble.

"The question is, are we going to let Charlie go back to Okeham Hall?"

"No way!"

Heidi gave Eva a serious look. "Not even if there's a good explanation?"

"Nope." As far as Eva was concerned, Jake and Marietta could never come up with a good enough reason to explain why they'd abandoned Charlie.

Before Heidi could reply they heard Mark calling for her from the yard.

"In the cattery!" Heidi called back.

Eva's dad joined them. "I just got back from the Brookses' place," he muttered, a dazed look on his face.

"That was a long visit," said Eva.

Mark scratched his head. "Yeah, I don't know what happened. I went to explain about our Open Day and before I knew it Linda Brooks was offering me coffee and Jason was going through all his old football scrapbooks with me."

"How come?" Eva asked.

"Does this mean peace has broken out?" Heidi said at the same time.

"Linda has found out about Jake Adams being our star guest tomorrow," Mark explained. "Don't ask me how. Anyway, she told Jason, and it turns out Jason is a massive fan."

"But—" Eva tried to interrupt.

Her dad cut her off. "I know, but listen. As soon as Jason heard, he convinced Linda that our Open Day was a good thing because it would mean lots of our pets would find new homes, and so this place would be a lot less crowded and noisy. Which means it'll be quieter for them in the near future."

"But—" Eva tried again.

"I know, can you believe it?" He sighed and spread his hands, palms upwards. "They said they might even drop by tomorrow to see Jake."

"But Jake isn't coming!" Eva pointed out at last.

Her dad frowned. "I know. But I couldn't get a word in edgeways, and in the end I just didn't have the heart to tell them!"

Chapter Seven

"So what's going to happen to you?"
Eva asked Charlie when she went to
visit him later that evening.

Charlie was snuggled up next to
Treacle, curled into a soft ball with his
white front paws tucked under his chin.
The tip of his ginger tail twitched as
Eva leaned in to stroke him.

"It's OK, I won't disturb you," she
murmured. "I'm just wondering what'll
happen now. I hope Mum doesn't let you

go back to Jake's place. I hope she lets us find you someone new."

Charlie let his top lids sink down over his bright green eyes and he fell into a snooze.

"But if they do send you back, you have to promise not to go for another swim!" Eva went on. "Remember, water and cats don't mix!"

Next to Charlie, Treacle opened his mouth and yawned. Over in the corner of the unit, Wilma and Snap were already fast asleep.

"Water – nasty, cold, wet stuff!" Eva insisted. "Brrr!"

Charlie opened one eye, and then closed it again.

"OK, I'll let you get some sleep." Eva smiled, giving him one last stroke.

There were so many problems to solve and questions hanging over the kitten's future, but now it was late and everyone was tired. "Goodnight, Treacle," she whispered. "Goodnight, Charlie. Sleep well!"

"Sleep well, Eva," her dad said as he'd turned off the light.

Eva lay on her back, staring up at the ceiling. She wasn't sleepy at all – her head was too busy worrying about Charlie and wondering why his new owners had let him down.

I don't get it! she thought over and over. Why would anyone adopt a kitten and then leave him home alone?

She remembered poor little Charlie

hiding among the big plant pots at
Okeham Hall.

He must have been hungry! she thought.
And lonely and scared!

When she finally drifted off, her
sleep was full of dreams about dark,
glittering swimming pools and empty
houses which had long, creepy corridors
with creaking doors and spooky,
whispering voices.

"Oh!" Eva woke up from her
nightmare. She pulled her duvet
tightly around her shoulders, gradually
realizing that daylight was already
filtering through her curtains. "Phew!"
She breathed a sigh of relief.

Throwing back her bedclothes, she
went to open the curtains. "Rain!" she
groaned, peering out. The yard was

covered in puddles, the slate roof of the surgery was shiny and water trickled along the gutters. She glanced up at the grey sky, which didn't look like clearing any time soon. "What a rotten start to our Open Day!"

Eva got dressed and went downstairs. She was halfway through her bowl of cereal before she looked at the clock and saw that it was only ten to six. No wonder no one else was up.

OK, so what do I do now? she wondered. *Go back to bed? No, I know – I could send one last email to Jake! Surely it's worth a try.*

She flung on her wellies and waterproof jacket and trotted across the yard to the surgery, where Joel Allerton was just finishing his night shift.

"What are you doing up so early?"
Joel asked Eva. He yawned and ran
his hand through his hair, checking off
medicines on the shelf against a list of
stock on the computer screen.

"Couldn't sleep," she said, logging
on to the computer next to Joel's. "Just
wanted to send an email!"

Eva brought up the message from Jake and the one that she and Karl had tried and failed to send. "Can Marietta still make it?" She tried again. Once more the mail server sent it back.

"No good," Eva muttered. She was over her disappointment and starting to get cross. "How come people you trust let you down?" she asked Joel.

"Which people?" Joel glanced at the screen. "Oh, you mean our local soccer legend? I guess something important came up for him."

"*This* is important!" Eva insisted, pointing at one of the Open Day leaflets. "And so is adopting a kitten!"

"Ah, you mean Charlie." Joel had been keeping an eye on the ginger kitten all night to make sure he'd settled back in with his brothers and sister. "I'm with you on that one!"

Eva nodded. "I want to know what's going on."

"We know what's going on," Joel pointed out. "Some big-shot sports star makes a spur-of-the-moment decision to adopt a cute kitten for his girlfriend. But a few days later she's bored with kitty and they get invited to a friend's Spanish villa or whatever. Then it's bye-bye, Charlie, hello sunbathing!"

"It's so not fair!" Eva muttered, feeling even more cross. She jumped up from the computer, making her own on-the-spot decision. "If you see Mum and Dad, tell them I won't be long."

Joel glanced up from his monitor. "Why, where are you going?"

"Out!" Eva announced. "Back to Okeham Hall, to find out why Jake and Marietta abandoned Charlie!"

Eva cycled through the rain. Drops fell from her helmet on to her cold cheeks. Her tights were soon soaked through. *No traffic*, she thought with relief, splashing through puddles. She noticed the wet cows in the fields, and a sad-looking horse poking its head over one of the hedges as she sped along the country road leading to the Hall.

But as she approached the wide gates, the morning silence was broken by the loud revving of a car's engine.

Eva braked and pulled into the grass verge. The sound of the engine grew louder and a small blue car shot out from Okeham Hall drive and headed her way with a roar and squeal of tyres.

"Hey!" Eva cried, catching sight of a dark-haired woman at the wheel.

The woman sped past without seeming to notice her.

"Charming!" Eva muttered, her heart in her mouth. "*And* she didn't even bother to press the button and close the gates!"

As the sports car disappeared down the road, Eva seized her chance and rode down the drive towards the big hall.

In the early morning rain the old house looked dark and spooky, just like the haunted house of her dream. Eva could easily picture ghosts floating down corridors and gazing down at her from the battlements.

Get a grip! she told herself as she
approached the wide front door. *And who
was that woman in the blue car? It wasn't
Marietta. And the car wasn't here when
Karl and I came yesterday. What on earth is
going on?*

Talking of cars, Eva thought it would be a good idea to check the garage. "If Jake and Marietta are away, their cars won't be here," she said out loud, skirting down the side of the house to peer through the small windows of an old stable block. To her surprise there were two cars parked inside. *Maybe they're back!* she thought.

She walked up to the front of the house and found the doorbell. *What now?* Eva wondered. Should she press it, or was it way too early to disturb Jake? Her finger hovered over the buzzer.

Then her gaze was drawn to a soggy piece of paper on the rain-spattered step. Eva stooped to pick it up. It was a smudged, hastily written message.

> Dear Bobbie,
>
> Please feed Charlie. Food is on the kitchen table.
> Leave him in laundry room with clean litter tray.
> Close door behind you. Back Sunday.
>
> Love Marietta x

Eva's eyes opened wide. She smoothed the note and read it again.

So Jake and Marietta hadn't dumped Charlie after all. They'd made a plan to have him looked after by someone called Bobbie. But it had all gone wrong.

Bobbie hadn't turned up when he should have done, and now Charlie was back at the rescue centre. Which left two big questions in Eva's mind. Who was the woman in the blue sports car? And why was she in such a hurry to get away?

Chapter Eight

By nine o'clock, the yard at Animal
Magic was buzzing with activity.

Eva watched people come and
go. She had said nothing about her
early morning visit to the Hall or the
mysterious blue car that had shot out of
the drive. She was still thinking about
it when she saw a Land Rover splash
through the puddles and enter the
yard. She waved and ran to greet her
grandad.

"Have you come to help?" she asked, as Jimmy Harrison climbed out of the car. Eva grabbed him by the hand, steering him past the biggest puddles.

"You bet!" he grinned.

"What about Gro-well?"

Eva and Karl's grandad ran a small garden centre on the outskirts of the village. You never saw him without his green gardening waistcoat and a pair of sharp secateurs stuffed in his pocket.

"I left Thomas in charge. He's been working for me long enough. I reckon he can manage by himself for one day." Still smiling, he waved at Mark and Karl. "When does the great man arrive?" he yelled. "Jake Adams is a real crowd-puller. Are you ready for the rush?"

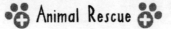

Eva bit her lip. "Grandad, didn't Dad tell you?"

"Tell me what?" Jimmy Harrison put on his flat cap and zipped up his waistcoat.

Eva broke the news bluntly. "Jake Adams isn't coming. He backed out at the last minute."

"Wow!" a voice from next door gasped. Annie's head appeared over the hedge. "Are you serious?"

Eva's shoulders sagged. "Jake can't come," she admitted. "Anyway, what are you doing, Annie? You're not supposed to listen to other people's conversations!"

"I can't help it if I happen to be in my garden!" Annie protested weakly.

"I'll leave you two to argue it out," Jimmy said, shaking his head and looking disappointed as he went off to find a job to do.

"You're *never* in your garden!" Eva tutted at Annie. "Especially when it's raining. You hate getting your hair wet!"

Annie ignored her. "What happened to Jake?"

"Don't ask me." Wiping the rain from her face, Eva realized it was no use being mad with Annie. "Sorry," she mumbled. "I know it's not your fault."

"No worries," Annie replied.

"Don't tell your dad," Eva pleaded. "He'll think we made it up – the stuff

73

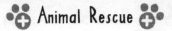

about Jake coming – just to stop your
mum from complaining about us."

Annie nodded. "OK, I won't say
anything. But he's going to find out
soon any—"

At that moment there was a blast
from a car horn in next door's drive, and
the sound of a car's tyres squealing to a
halt.

"Oops!" Annie turned in time to see
her mum stop sharply at the exit from
their drive.

Out of the corner of her eye, Eva saw
a second car on Main Street. The driver
jammed on the brakes. "That was
close!" she breathed.

The second car swerved, then crunched
into the lamp post outside Annie's
house.

"Ouch!" Eva grimaced. She saw Karl sprint across the yard towards the road and she quickly followed. By the time they reached the gate, Linda Brooks was already out of her car and standing on the pavement, while a dark-haired woman stepped shakily out of her small blue car.

"What do you think you're doing?!" Linda shrieked. "This is a thirty mile per hour zone! You must have been doing at least fifty!"

"Are you OK?" Karl asked the woman, noting her front bumper bent around the lamp post and a hiss of steam emerging from under the bonnet.

Soon other people came running, including Mark Harrison, who quickly took control. "Karl, can you go down the street and try to warn drivers that there's been an accident. Get them to slow down."

Karl nodded and hurried off. Eva stayed at her dad's side. She'd recognized the crashed car – it was the same one that she'd seen at Okeham Hall.

"Linda, are you OK?" Mark checked. Then he turned back to the other driver. "You've probably had a bit of a shock. Would you like to come inside while we try to sort your car out for you?"

"Don't touch the car!" Linda insisted. "I'm going to call the police. They'll have to measure braking distances before it gets towed away."

Sighing, Mark led the woman towards the house.

"I wasn't breaking the speed limit." The young woman spoke for the first time. "Your neighbour shot out from her driveway without looking. I had to swerve to avoid her."

Hearing this, Eva frowned. She'd seen how fast the woman had come out of the drive at Okeham Hall a few hours earlier. But she didn't say anything.

"I'm so sorry to bother you," the woman went on, sitting down in the kitchen and accepting a cup of tea. "It looks as if you're very busy."

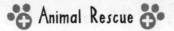

"No problem," Mark assured her.
"Stay here. Eva will keep you company.
I'll go outside and wait for the police."

Nodding, the woman took a deep
breath and sipped her tea.

"Did you come to Okeham for a
reason?" Eva asked carefully, her
curiosity bubbling over in spite of the
shock of the accident.

The woman looked pale and worried.
She was young, with long, glossy brown
hair. "I went to my sister's house, but
she wasn't in."

"Whereabouts?"

The woman glanced cautiously at
Eva. "It doesn't matter. Never mind."

She's hiding something! Eva thought.
But there was no time to ask more
questions, because her dad reappeared

with a police officer who immediately
asked to see the woman's driving
licence.

"Roberta Jarvis," the policeman said,
reading the name on the licence and
writing it down. "Now, Miss Jarvis, how
fast were you driving at the time of the
accident?"

"Mum's gone mental!" Annie reported to Eva an hour after the policeman had left. "She's denying coming out of the drive without looking and she's saying that Roberta Jarvis was doing fifty!"

"Well, I heard Roberta tell the police that she was under the speed limit," Eva replied.

"Eva, can you check the hay in Rosie and Apache's nets?" Heidi called from the surgery door.

Eva started towards the stables. "See you later," she told Annie. As she crossed the yard, her dad appeared at the back door with Roberta. He hurried over to Jimmy Harrison, who was helping Karl put up some bunting.

"Dad, could you give Roberta a lift?"
he asked. "Her car's not driveable and
she needs to get home."

"Of course." Jimmy smiled kindly
at the pale young woman. "Where's
home?"

"In Hareton," she explained with a
hesitant smile. "I'm sorry to put you to
all this trouble."

"No problem," he assured her. "It's
only a couple of miles."

Hearing this, Eva dashed on into the
stable to check on the pony's feed, and
then hurried back out. "I'll go with
Grandad," she told her dad.

No sooner said than Eva climbed into
the back seat of the Land Rover with
Roberta. Jimmy pulled out from the
yard and switched on the radio.

"Sorry!" Roberta said again, seemingly on the verge of tears.

Jimmy drove on past her smashed car without replying.

"He didn't hear you. He's a bit deaf," Eva explained. "I saw you earlier," she said quietly.

Roberta shot her a worried look. "Where?"

Eva looked her in the eye. "At Jake Adams's place."

Roberta frowned. "Why were you snooping around there?"

"I was going to ask you that," Eva retorted. "Come on, you tell me first."

"I was looking for a cat," Roberta sighed. "A kitten actually. It belongs to my sister."

It was Eva's turn to frown. "Marietta?"

Roberta nodded. "She and Jake had to go away all of a sudden."

"Marietta's your sister?"

"Yes. She asked me to look after her kitten. But it escaped from the house and ran off."

Hang on a second! Eva tried to fit the pieces together. True, Marietta and Jake had had a sudden change of plan. But hadn't she found the note addressed to a man called Bobbie, asking him to take care of Charlie? That didn't make sense!

"I came to the Hall at midday yesterday," Roberta went on. "I only opened the back door a little way, but Charlie shot out between my legs and vanished!"

"Charlie!" Eva echoed. *Roberta —*

Bobbie. Bobbie's not a man – she's a woman!

"I came back twice in the afternoon to look for him, but he never showed up," Bobbie explained. "And I got up early this morning and came over first thing. And again just after nine. Still no luck. Poor little Charlie has vanished into thin air. I've no idea what I'm going to tell Marietta when she gets back!"

Chapter Nine

"Grandad, turn round!" Eva cried. She leaned forward and tapped his shoulder. "Take us back to Animal Magic, please!"

"Make up your mind," her grandad grumbled.

Bobbie turned to Eva with a puzzled look. "What's up? Why are we going back?"

Eva took a deep breath. Suddenly everything looked different. "There's

been a big mistake!" she gasped. "Karl and I ... we thought ... well, anyway, you'll soon see!"

Jimmy Harrison turned the car around and set off back to the rescue centre.

"My brother and I wanted to find out why Jake had changed his mind about coming to our Open Day," Eva told Bobbie. "He promised to be here, but then he backed out. That's why we went to Okeham Hall yesterday afternoon."

"Uh-oh, Eva, what have you been up to this time?" her grandad asked.

"The house was empty ... and, well ... we thought poor little Charlie had been left without anyone to look after him."

Bobbie nodded. "OK, I get it. But actually I was the one who messed up in the first place by letting Charlie escape.

He ran off and I couldn't get him to come back. I didn't know what to do!"

"Here we are, girls!" Jimmy announced, pulling into the yard at Animal Magic.

"Come on!" Eva urged Marietta's confused sister. She led her towards the cattery and headed straight for the unit containing Charlie and his brothers and sister. "Excuse me," she murmured to a couple of visitors who were gazing at the adorable litter. Then she leaned over and picked up the snuggly, fluffy ginger kitten.

"Charlie!" Bobbie gasped in total amazement. "Oh, Charlie, there you are! Thank heavens!"

"Am I in trouble?" Eva asked her mum as Bobbie cuddled Charlie.

Straight away, Bobbie stood up for Eva. "Oh, please don't tell her off! She did what she thought was best. And she saved Charlie from drowning, remember!"

"Actually, that was Karl," Eva admitted. Her brother hovered in the background, ready to do a runner if things turned nasty.

"You're right, Bobbie." Heidi nodded. She reached out and stroked Charlie. "All's well that ends well."

Phew! Eva relaxed and Karl sidled up, smiling, hands in his pockets.

"Thank you so much!" Bobbie said to him. "You saved Charlie's life!"

"Do you happen to know why Jake had

to cancel our Open Day?" Karl asked.
"We're going to look really stupid when
Mum has to make the announcement
that he won't be here after all."

"I'm sorry, I really don't know."
Bobbie held tight to Charlie and walked
with Heidi, Eva and Karl out into
the yard. There was a distant roll of
thunder and heavy splashes of rain. Wet
visitors scuttled from the kennels to the
cattery, and on into the converted barn
that held the rabbits and guinea pigs.
"I can't help you. I wish I could."

"Didn't Marietta tell you?" Eva asked.

Bobbie shook her head. "Listen, can
I call a taxi? I have to get Charlie back
to Okeham Hall. And this time, I'll
make dead sure he doesn't get out of
the house!"

Eva's grandad overheard and stepped forward. "No need for a taxi. I'll run you there. As long as you don't change your mind again halfway!"

No sooner said than Eva, Bobbie and Charlie were back in the Land Rover.

"So Marietta didn't explain where she and Jake were going?" Eva prompted again, as they set off for the Hall.

"I thought it was a bit weird at the

time," Bobbie confessed. "Marietta seemed upset when she phoned me and told me they had to go away. She wouldn't explain – just asked me to look after Charlie."

There was a short silence, and then Bobbie went on. "If you ask me, it was to do with the Angela Nixon fiasco."

"Who's she?" Eva asked.

"She is – no, she was until recently – Jake's Personal Assistant. She lived at the Hall with Jake and Marietta. But my sister found out on Thursday that Angela had been fiddling her expenses and Jake fired her on the spot."

"But what's that got to do with Jake having to leave unexpectedly?" Eva didn't see it, and Bobbie had no real answers for her.

"I don't know – just a feeling," she murmured.

They lapsed into silence again as Jimmy turned into the drive of Okeham Hall and drove slowly through the still-open gates towards the big old house.

"Home again!" Bobbie said to Charlie as she unlocked the front door.

The ginger kitten sniffed and wriggled. Bobbie put him down gently and watched him stick his pointy tail straight up in the air and pad carefully across the polished floor.

Meow! Charlie said, heading for the kitchen.

"Maybe he's hungry," Bobbie mused, inviting Eva and Jimmy into the house.

"Thirsty, more like." Eva knew that the kittens had already been fed. She smiled to see Charlie lap greedily at the saucer of water that Bobbie put down.

Bobbie's phone went and she hurried to answer it.

"Marietta!" she said, walking quickly out of the kitchen, and into the hall.

Eva couldn't hear what was being said, but she could tell that Bobbie sounded surprised. "Maybe now we'll find out what happened to Jake," she said glumly to her grandad. They waited for Bobbie to return.

"I knew it!" Bobbie frowned, pacing up and down the big kitchen. "It is Angela Nixon! I knew she was bad news. Not only does she deliberately crash Jake's computer when she finds out she's been sacked, she sends him off for a big meeting with United's boss which hasn't even been arranged!"

Eva's grandad whistled gently. "Not Mark Moorcroft himself!"

Bobbie took a deep breath. "Yes, the big boss. Apparently Angela said Moorcroft needed to talk to Jake about renewing his contract. She made it seem like his future at the club was in doubt and got him to drive all the way to United's ground, only to find there was no meeting after all. Moorcroft didn't show up, and it turns out he's on holiday with his family in Florida."

"Wow! That's mean!" Suddenly a new thought flashed into her head. "Where are Jake and Marietta now?"

"On their way home."

"On their way home!" Eva echoed. "Wow, Bobbie, that's cool! Did they say…? I mean, can you call them back? Find out if…"

Jimmy stepped in with a smile to help Eva out. "I think what my excited granddaughter is trying to say is, will you ask Jake if he'll be back in time to put in an appearance at our Open Day?"

Chapter Ten

It was after one o'clock when Eva and her grandfather arrived back at Animal Magic.

"Remember, say nothing to your mum and dad about Jake," Jimmy said, holding the car door open for Eva to jump out.

Back at the Hall, Bobbie had promised Eva that she would call Marietta back, but she had warned them not to place too much hope on the celebrity couple being back in time. "I wouldn't want you to be disappointed all over again," she'd told Eva.

Even so, Eva's brown eyes were sparkling with excitement, and it was almost more than she could bear. *Jake, be here!* she begged silently. *Please be here! Everyone's still expecting you. Don't let us down!*

Meanwhile, visitors crowded into the yard. There was a buzz of conversation as people went from kennels to cattery to stables, and all the talk was about the soccer superstar.

"Where's Jake Adams…? He's not due until two… It's good of him to support an animal rescue centre… I reckon he's a really nice bloke!"

Eva followed a family of two parents

and two kids into the stables where
Rosie and Apache munched hay.

"Look at the little brown pony, Mum!"
the girl cried. "It says on the label that
her name's Rosie. How sweet is she!"

"Gorgeous," the woman agreed. "I had
a pony just like her when I was your
age."

Eva grinned and crossed her fingers.
She moved on to the dog kennels, where
a young couple were looking at Becks.

"Beautiful!" the woman sighed,
bending down to the Great Dane's eye
level. "These dogs have lovely, gentle
natures in spite of their size. Oh, Ben,
wouldn't it be great to give Becks a
home!"

Fingers crossed! Eva smiled and went on,
past Penny's and Bruno's kennels. This

could work out brilliantly – if only Jake
Adams could make it here in time!

"Hello, Eva!" Outside in the yard once
more, she heard Annie's dad call her
name. "Where's Jake? Is he here yet?"

Eva took a deep breath and held
back her answer. "I don't know. Better
ask Mum!" *Phew!* She breathed a sigh

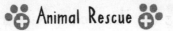
of relief as Jason dashed on. Then she spotted Annie hanging about by herself outside the cattery.

"What a day!" Eva said, starting to tell Annie about Charlie. "He hadn't been left home alone after all! You know the woman in the blue sports car who ran into the lamp post? Well, it turns out she—"

"Stop!" Annie pleaded. She shook her head unhappily. "Didn't Dad tell you?"

"No. What?"

"About the accident. The police got back in touch. It looks like the woman in the blue car—"

"Bobbie," Eva interrupted. "Roberta, shortened to Bobbie."

"Yes, whatever. Well, it looks like she was doing under thirty miles an hour after all. And it was Mum who drove out without looking."

"Whoa!" Eva stared at her friend.

"I know. Mum's in floods of tears. I expect she'll have to apologize to Roberta." Annie predicted that the next few days at home were going to be tough. "We don't know yet if the police will charge her."

"Wow!" Eva took a step back. "Hey, look, the sun just came out!"

"Just in time for me to make my announcement about Jake," Heidi muttered as she passed by with Mark. "I'm not looking forward to this!"

Eva glanced at her watch and saw that it was almost two o'clock. *OK, I guess it was too much to hope for,* she told herself. *It would have been like a little piece of pure magic if Jake had shown up in time!*

Still expecting the soccer star to appear through the door, the crowd of visitors gathered round. Eva spotted Jason Brooks and Karl's friend, George Stevens, along with a hundred other eager faces. This was the moment they had all been waiting for. "Oh no, poor Mum having to tell them!" she groaned.

"Ladies and gentlemen, thank you for coming," Heidi began. "We're delighted that so many of you have turned up to see the work we do here at Animal Magic."

Heidi smiled at the excited crowd and took a deep breath. "Unfortunately…"

But just as Eva hung her head, dreading her mum's next words, a car drove into the yard and came to a halt.

All heads turned. The driver's door opened and Jake Adams stepped out.

A big cheer went up as everyone turned to greet the great man. Heidi Harrison stood outside her surgery door, wearing a look of stunned surprise.

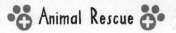

Thank you! Eva clasped her hands together and jumped up and down on the spot.

"Jake, can I have your autograph! … Jake, write on this cup-final programme! … Jake, you're the best striker United ever had!"

As the crowd swamped Jake Adams, Bobbie got out of the car with Marietta. They saw Eva and beckoned her across. "You're a total star!" Marietta told her. "Bobbie has told me everything you and Karl did for Charlie."

Eva grinned and blushed, unable to think of a thing to say. In any case, she saw that Jake had finally escaped from his fans and was standing by the surgery door, ready to make a speech. He looked shy and uncomfortable, waiting for the noise to die down.

"I just want to say what a great place this is," Jake began. "Heidi and her team are doing a brilliant job, and all the animals that end up at Animal Magic are extremely lucky. I just wish there were more centres like this."

"Yeah!" Eva said, along with a lot of other people in the crowd.

"They need your support," Jake went on, "so now that you're here, why don't you stick around and adopt a pet, like we did? Go on, do it. Show that you care!"

"Cool!" Eva cried, clapping loudly, and then cheering as Jake disappeared inside the surgery. "We love you, Jake!" she yelled. "We so love you. We really do!"

Chapter Eleven

"We've found new homes for three rabbits and two guinea pigs," Mark said.

Karl clicked his mouse and brought up the details on the Animal Magic website. He put ticks next to pictures of the pets who had been adopted.

"We also found owners for six dogs, including Penny, Bruno and Becks," Joel reported.

"Brilliant!" Eva nodded happily. "And

what about Rosie?"

"Maybe," Joel said. "It depends
what we find out about her present
owners when they come back from their
holiday. If it turns out the way we want
it to, she'll go to the Boswells, because
they can offer her a lovely new home."

"Cool." Their Open Day had worked
out perfectly – better than even Eva
could have hoped.

"Best of all, in the cattery we matched
nine cats with new owners," Heidi told
everyone. "Wilma and Snap both went
to a very nice retired lady in town."

"Oh, poor Treacle," Eva whispered.
"That means he's left here by himself."

Karl clicked and ticked. "That's
twenty-one animals altogether," he said.
"How cool is that!"

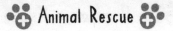
"Twenty-two!" a voice said, and they all turned to see Bobbie, Jake and Marietta standing in the doorway.

Karl counted again. "Three plus two plus six plus one plus nine. That makes twenty-one," he insisted.

But Bobbie came forward holding a squirming tabby kitten in her hands. "I'd like to adopt Treacle," she said. "If you think I'll be a good owner, that is."

Heidi looked at Eva. "What do you think?"

Eva went up to Bobbie and took Treacle from her. She cuddled him close. "I think you'll be perfect!" she said to Bobbie. She was sure Bobbie would care for him and feed him and keep him safe. "You know Dad found him in an air vent behind a factory?"

Bobbie, Jake and Marietta listened to the whole story as Eva took Treacle out into the warm sunshine.

"Dad works for a parcel delivery company. He was in the factory car park when he heard a meowing sound coming from the air vent, so he went to take a look…"

Karl, Heidi and Mark stood in the doorway watching Eva chatter to their guests.

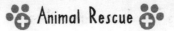

"So cool!" Karl sighed, staring at Jake and suffering from a serious case of hero worship.

"A good day!" Heidi said, bringing out a cardboard pet carrier for the kitten. Animal Magic had done its job.

Eva popped Treacle into the carrier and took him over to Jake's car.

"He's been microchipped, and he's had his jabs," Eva assured Bobbie. "No need to worry about that."

As Jake started the engine, Marietta leaned out of the window. "Thanks, Eva!"

Eva nodded and smiled. Her dad came to join her and put his arm around her shoulder.

"Give me a shout any time you need me," Jake told him as he pushed the car into gear.

As they watched the soccer star leave
the yard, Eva looked up at her dad.
"OK," she said, her eyes sparkling,
a grin splitting her face from ear to
ear. "When do we have our next mega
Animal Magic Open Day?!"

Have you read...

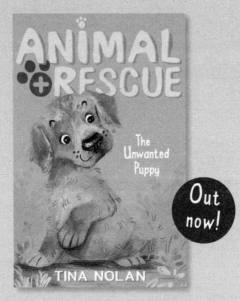

The Unwanted Puppy

Out now!

TINA NOLAN

Coming soon!

The Homeless Foal

TINA NOLAN

The Injured Fox Cub

TINA NOLAN